On the journey to the town.

The wheels on the bus go round and round
Over dusty ground, over dusty ground.
The wheels on the bus go round and round

Town

The Wheels on the Bus

Illustrated by
Melanie Williamson
Sung by The Amador Family

Barefoot Books
step inside a story

The bus starts up with a rumble and crunch.
The driver calls out, "We'll be there by lunch."
The bus starts up with a rumble and a crunch

TOWN

BUS 1

On the journey to the town.

The children on the bus all shout and play
Along the way, along the way.
The children on the bus all shout and play

On the journey to the town.

The papis stand up to sing and hum,
Bang a drum, bang a drum.
The papis stand up to sing and hum

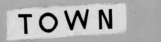

On the journey to the town.

The babies on the bus all start to cry,
Bouncing low, bouncing high.
The babies on the bus all start to cry

On the journey to the town.

The wheel on the bus goes

BANG!

A granny at the back says, "Never fear,
Granny's here, Granny's here!"
A granny at the back says, "Never fear!"

On the journey to the town.

The mamis on the bus have found a spare,
"It's over there, it's over there."
The mamis on the bus have found a spare

On the journey to the town.

The people on the street help lift it high,
More stop by, more stop by.
The people on the street help lift it high

On the journey to the town.

The wheels on the bus go round again,
Thank you, friends; thank you, friends.
The wheels on the bus go round again

All the way
to town!

Guatemala

This book is set in Guatemala, in Central America.

Physical Features

Guatemala is a small, tropical country and a
land of jungles, mountains and mountain lakes.
On its coasts are coral reefs and volcanic beaches.
The only flat region is near the coast.

GUATEMALA

Markets

Markets are an important part of life in Guatemala.
Every week, people travel from villages and farms to trade
at their local market. Market day is like a fiesta (a party)
or a holiday. All kinds of goods are sold, among them eggs,
corn, tomatoes, birds, animals and hand-woven items such
as blouses, trousers, hats and shawls.

Chicken Buses

People often travel to market on "chicken buses"
like the bus in this book. These buses are
usually old American school buses enjoying
a brightly painted new life in Guatemala!

Weaving

Guatemalan women wear a blouse called a *huipil*. This pretty, woven blouse has traditional patterns sewn onto it in bright rainbow threads. Each village has its own unique patterns and threads. Weaving is an important part of life in Guatemala.

Money

Guatemalan money is named after a bird – the quetzal. The Maya were the first people to live in Guatemala and they used the quetzal's bright and gaudy feathers as currency. The Resplendent Quetzal is the Guatemalan national bird.

Guatemalan Flag

The Guatemalan flag has three stripes: white in the middle with two light blue stripes on either side.

The blue stripes represent the Pacific Ocean to the west and Caribbean Sea to the east of Guatemala. The white stripe symbolizes peace and purity.

The Wheels on the Bus

Bouncy and fun ♩ = 140

The bus starts up with a rum-ble and a crunch. The dri-ver calls out, "We'll be there by lunch" The

bus starts up with a rum-ble and a crunch, on the jour-ney to the town.

Barefoot Books, 2067 Massachusetts Ave, Cambridge, MA 02140
Barefoot Books, 29/30 Fitzroy Square, London, W1T 6LQ

Text adaptation copyright © 2014 by Stella Blackstone • Illustrations copyright © 2014 by Melanie Williamson
The moral rights of Stella Blackstone and Melanie Williamson have been asserted
Lead vocals by Brian Amador • Background vocals by Rosi Amador • Additional vocals by Zia and Alisa Amador
Musical arrangement © 2014 by Brian Amador, Greñudo Music (BMI) • Guitar, tres, percussion and MIDI programming by Brian Amador
Recorded, mixed and mastered by Brian Amador • Animation by Sophie Marsh and Thomas Barth, Bristol, England • Photoshop by Sarita McNeil

First published in Great Britain by Barefoot Books, Ltd and in the United States of America by Barefoot Books, Inc in 2014

Graphic design by Bianca Lucas, Busy Bee Press, England
Reproduction by B & P International, Hong Kong • Printed in China on 100% acid-free paper
This book was typeset in Carrot Cake and Centaur • The illustrations were prepared in acrylic, pencils and chalk

Hardback with enhanced CD ISBN 978-1-84686-787-3 • Paperback with enhanced CD ISBN 978-1-84686-788-0

British Cataloguing-in-Publication Data: a catalogue record for this book is available from the British Library

Library of Congress Cataloging-in-Publication Data is available under LCCN 2013024827

9

Go to *www.barefootbooks.com/wheelsonbus* to access
your audio singalong and video animation online.